Spotter's Guide to
THE NIGHT SKY

Nigel Henbest MSc FRAS

Illustrated by

With thanks to Sue

Star charts by Studio

USBORNE

This is a view through a telescope of the Great Nebula in the constellation of Orion. See where to look for it on page 19; mark it off when you have spotted it (page 27).

Contents

First published in 1979 by
Usborne Publishing Ltd,
83-85 Saffron Hill,
London EC1N 8RT.

© 1992, 1985, 1979 by Usborne
Publishing Ltd.

Printed in Great Britain

Universal Edition

The name Usborne and the device are
Trade Marks of Usborne Publishing Ltd.

How to use this book

Stars

These are just some of the things you can see in the night skies

Planet

Comet

The Moon

Aurora

This book is an identification guide to the wide range of things you can see in the sky at night. Take it with you when you go out spotting on a clear night. Not all the objects in this book can be seen on any one night, but during the year you should be able to spot most of those visible from where you live.

Some objects, like the stars, are very distant, while the planets, comets and the Moon are much closer, though even the Moon is a long way away – over 380,000 km. A few of the 'lights' in the night sky, like the aurorae, occur in the Earth's atmosphere. This book starts with distant sky sights and then moves to ones closer to Earth with descriptions to help you identify them.

Read through the book inside the house before you go out, so you know roughly the kinds of things to look out for – how to recognize a satellite, for example. Find out which constellations are visible, using the sky map on page 8 (or page 10 if you live in the southern hemisphere). Look to see where the planets will be, and if there will be any meteor showers.

Next to most of the things in the book is a small blank circle. Each time you spot an object, make a mark in the circle. Some things, like the more distant planets, can only be seen with powerful telescopes so these do not have circles to mark next to them.

Scorecard

At the end of the book is a scorecard which gives you a score for each object you spot. A common or easily recognized object scores 5 points; a very rare or faint one is worth up to 50 points. You can add up your score after a night's spotting, or at the end of each week.

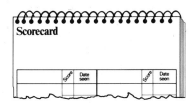

Scorecard

| | Score | Date seen | | Score | Date seen |

Observing the skies

When you go out star-spotting remember to dress warmly. Even in summer you will get cold quickly when sitting still, and in winter you will need to wear two pairs of socks, two sweaters, a warm hat and gloves. Some astronomers even wear two pairs of trousers, one over the other.

A deckchair is a comfortable and convenient place to sit while observing the sky. Standing up soon becomes uncomfortable, and if you lie on the ground you may end up wet from dew or frost. A mat will keep your feet warmer if they touch the ground when you are sitting. Choose a spot in your garden where your sky-view is not blocked by trees, and, if you can, keep away from street lights.

When you come out of a brightly lit house into a dark night, your eyes will take about half an hour to adjust to the dark. At first you will see just the brighter stars, so wait a little before searching for the fainter objects. To keep your eyes dark-adapted, use a red or a very dim light to read this book while observing. Bright light will make your eyes much less sensitive.

Don't have a hot drink before you go out, because it will, surprisingly, soon make you feel cold. Have one when you come in to warm up, especially if you are going straight to bed.

Hat

Socks

Thick trousers

Coat

Thick shoes

Two pullovers

Gloves

Torch lens covered with red acetate

Binoculars and telescopes

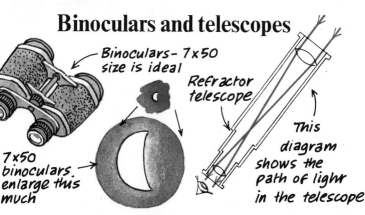

Binoculars - 7x50 size is ideal

7x50 binoculars enlarge this much

Refractor telescope

This diagram shows the path of light in the telescope

You can see most of the sky sights in this book with your unaided eyes, but a pair of binoculars will show you much more.

Binoculars are just a pair of telescopes, one for each eye. Telescopes magnify objects, and so they show you more detail than the eye alone can see. A reasonable pair of binoculars (7 x 50 are ideal) will reveal craters on the Moon, and the round globe of Jupiter.

Unfortunately binoculars will also magnify the shaking of your hands as you hold them, and the image will wobble about.

The large front lenses of binoculars gather much more light than your eyes, so the view through binoculars is very bright. Some stars are quite dazzling, and the binoculars will show you many stars which are too faint for your unaided eyes to see.

A telescope is more powerful than binoculars, but more expensive, and many of the cheaper ones are of rather poor quality. Generally it is better to buy a pair of binoculars than a cheap telescope at the same price, if you have the choice. The pictures above and below show the two types of telescope you could use. The refractor uses glass lenses to refract (or bend) the light. The reflector uses a mirror for the same purpose.

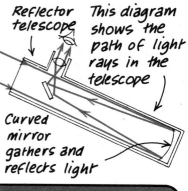

Reflector telescope

This diagram shows the path of light rays in the telescope

Curved mirror gathers and reflects light

Our place in the Universe

Sun Mercury Venus

North Pole   Day

Night   Sun's rays

The Earth rotates once every 23 hours 56 minutes

The Earth is one of nine planets which go around the Sun in circular paths, called orbits. You can see above a diagram of the Solar System, which is the name for the Sun, planets, comets and asteroids.

The Earth turns around once a day and completes one revolution around the Sun in a year. Keeping the Earth company is the Moon, a much smaller body, which circles the Earth once every 27 days. It is the Earth's only natural satellite, although since 1957 thousands of artificial satellites have been launched by rocket to circle the Earth. Most of the other planets have natural satellites, and Saturn holds the record with seventeen of them.

Although the planets and the Moon shine brightly in the sky, they are only reflecting light from the Sun; they do not produce their own light. The Sun is the bright yellow one at the top of the picture.

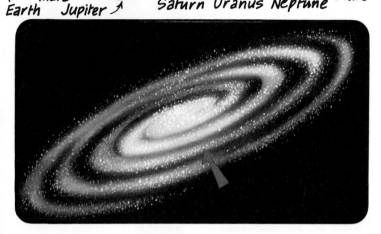

Earth Asteroids Mars Jupiter Saturn Uranus Neptune Pluto

The picture above shows the Milky Way galaxy, a vast spiral of stars and dust of which the Solar System is a member. Astronomers think that there are about 100,000 million stars in the galaxy. The red arrow shows the position of the Solar System, though on this scale, the Sun is too tiny to be made out.

Distances between stars are vast and are measured in light years, the distance that light travels in a year. Light speed is just under 300,000 kilometres a second, so a light year (LY) is about 10 million million kilometres. The nearest star, Proxima Centauri, is 4.3LY away, while the galaxy is 100,000LY across.

Beyond our galaxy, which you can see in the night sky as a faint band of light called the Milky Way, are billions of others extending into the furthest depths of space. The nearest are the two Magellanic Clouds, visible in the southern hemisphere. They are between 170,000 and 200,000LY away.

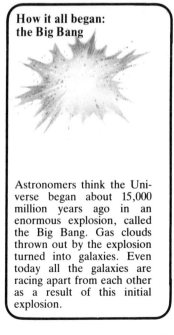

How it all began: the Big Bang

Astronomers think the Universe began about 15,000 million years ago in an enormous explosion, called the Big Bang. Gas clouds thrown out by the explosion turned into galaxies. Even today all the galaxies are racing apart from each other as a result of this initial explosion.

Stars of the northern skies

On a clear night you can see about 3,000 stars scattered across the sky. Astronomers find their way around by grouping stars together into patterns, like join-the-dot puzzles. These 88 patterns, called constellations, are always known by their Latin names; most were first named thousands of years ago.

During the night, the sky seems to rotate, carrying the constellations slowly from east to west. In fact, it is the Earth which is turning, causing some constellations to rise and others to set.

You see different constellations at different times of the year as the Earth moves around the Sun. Also, people in the northern hemisphere cannot see the stars above the South Pole and vice versa, because of the Earth's spherical shape.

The sky map on the right shows the brightest stars visible from the northern hemisphere. The stars to be seen from the southern hemisphere are on page 10.

How to use the star map

Find the month in the map margin; turn the book around until the current month is lowest. Sitting in your deckchair, face south and look for the stars as they appear on the map. You will be able to see most of the stars shown in the centre and lower part of the map.

Spot the prominent constellations, then turn to the page numbers marked to find the fainter constellations which are not marked here. The dashed lines show the areas covered by each double-page constellation map. The two small pictures show how the view changes over the year. The

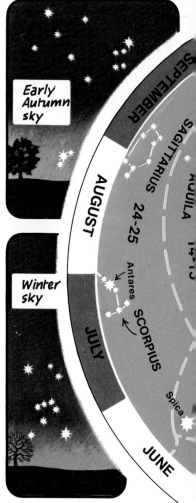

stars to be seen from one place in autumn, for example, are completely different from those seen from the same place in winter.

Signposts in the sky

Extend the imaginary lines joining the stars in the directions shown by the yellow arrows, to pinpoint bright stars and other constellations.

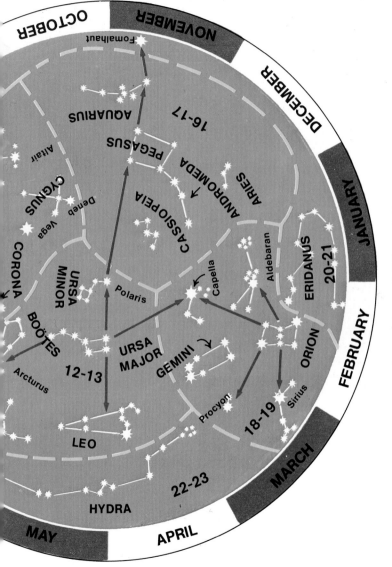

Stars of the southern skies

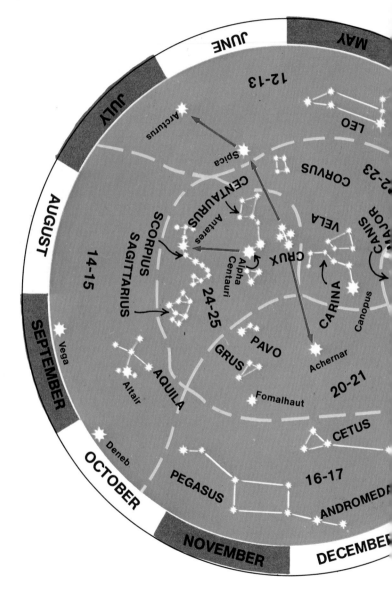

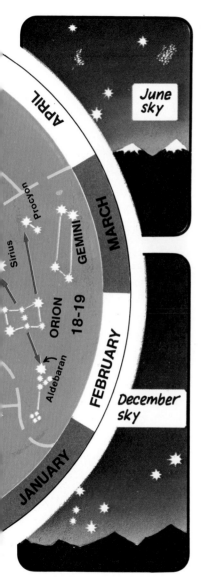

If you live in the southern hemisphere, use the map on the left to find your way around the skies. Turn the map until the present month is lowest. When you sit facing north you will be able to spot most of the stars shown in the centre and lower part of the map.

When you look at Sagittarius, you are also looking toward the centre of the galaxy, so you will see lots of stars in that area of the sky.

To the south you can see the southern cross, Crux. It can be used as a 'signpost' to other constellations, as shown by the yellow arrows.

When you have found the prominent constellations shown here, turn to the page numbers marked on the map. The areas covered by each detailed map are separated by dashed lines.

How to use the star charts on the following pages

Start by identifying the brightest stars and most prominent constellations. The size of the star symbols shows how bright each star is, not its actual size. You may have to tilt the maps to match them up with the sky. When you have recognized the obvious constellations, start looking for the fainter ones. It will probably take several nights before you know the sky well enough to spot them all.

Note that all the patterns will seem bigger in the sky than they appear on the maps. The two small views on the left show how the view of the sky changes at a particular spot through the year.

Draco to Cancer

1 Draco (dragon)

Long, straggling line of faint stars. Its 'head' is a group of four stars near Vega; the 'tail' loops around Ursa Minor. 4,700 years ago, Thuban was the pole star; today it is Polaris.

2 Canes Venatici (hunting dogs)

A constellation named in 1690. The 'dogs' hunt the 'bears' following them across the sky.

3 Boötes (herdsman)

A conspicuous kite-shape. Arcturus is the fourth brightest star in the sky: find it by using the curved handle of the Plough as a pointer.

4 Coma Berenices (Berenice's hair)

A cloud of faint stars; binoculars will show about 30.

5 Virgo (virgin)

A constellation representing the goddess of justice. Five stars form an obvious 'bowl'; Spica is a hot bright white star. Its name means 'ear of corn'.

Vega
(links to map, page 15)

Thuban

Alcor

Mizar

To Arcturus

Arcturus

Spica

Polaris, the pole star

6 Ursa Minor (little bear)

Mostly faint stars, but Polaris, the pole star, is important to navigators because it is always due north. It is over 300LY away.

7 Ursa Major (great bear)

A large constellation, whose 7 brightest stars make the 'Plough'. The two right-hand Plough stars, Dubhe and Merak, point to the pole star.

8 Lynx

A line of faint stars, so named because only the lynx-eyed can see it.

9 Leo Minor (small lion)

A faint constellation, named in 1690 by German astronomer Johann Hevelius.

10 Cancer (crab)

Faint stars between Leo and Gemini. The distant star cluster Praesepe (beehive) appears as a dim blur to the eye, but is spectacular through binoculars.

11 Leo (lion)

One of the few constellations which looks anything like what it is named after, in this case a crouching lion.

North celestial pole

The Plough

Kocab

Dubhe

Merak

Denebola

Praesepe

Regulus

Two end stars point to Polaris

13

Cygnus to Serpens

12 Cygnus (swan)

The bright star Deneb forms one corner of the summer triangle together with Vega and Altair. Binoculars show many faint stars in Cygnus.

13 Delphinus (dolphin)

A compact constellation, with a very distinctive shape. Its 'tail' star is 270 LY away.

14 Sagitta (arrow)

Four faint stars make an arrow shape, between Cygnus and Aquila.

'Summer triangle', visible in northern hemisphere in summer; in southern hemisphere, winter

Deneb

Albireo

Altair →

Giedi

15 Capricornus (goat)

A distorted triangle of faint stars. Giedi is a double star. You should just be able to make them out. The planet Neptune was in Capricornus when discovered.

16 Aquila (eagle)

The bright star Altair is easily recognized because of its two fainter flanking stars.

17 Scutum (shield)

Faint constellation, visible against a background of the Milky Way.

18 Vulpecula (fox)

A very inconspicuous star group; originally called the fox and goose.

21 Hercules

A large constellation, but rather shapeless and difficult to recognize.

19 Lyra (lyre)

Small but easily spotted group. Vega is the fifth brightest star in the sky and 26 LY distant.

22 Corona Borealis (northern crown)

A semicircle of faint stars between Vega and Arcturus.

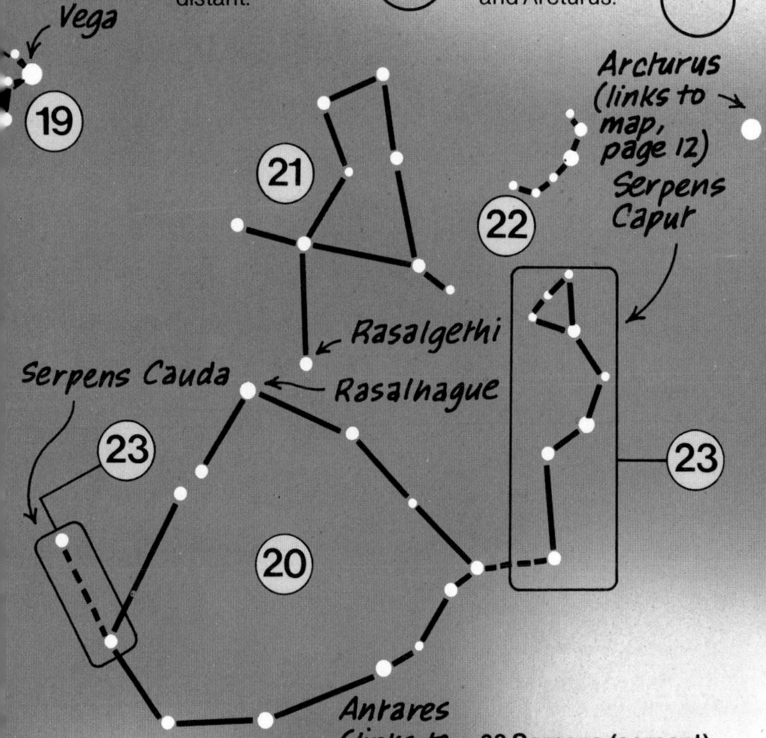

Vega

19

21

Arcturus
(links to
map,
page 12)

22

Serpens
Caput

Rasalgethi

Rasalhague

Serpens Cauda

23

23

20

Antares
(links to
map,
page 25)

20 Ophiuchus (serpent bearer)

A very large group of stars forming a distorted circle.

23 Serpens (serpent)

Consists of two separate parts: Caput (head) and Cauda (tail), lying either side of Ophiuchus.

Camelopardalis to Aquarius

24 Camelopardalis
(giraffe)
Just two major stars make up this constellation, first named in the 17th century.

25 Perseus
Named after a Greek hero. Algol is two stars close together – a binary. As one passes in front of the other, Algol fades to about half its normal brightness.

26 Andromeda
According to myth, a princess rescued by Perseus. The Andromeda galaxy, 2.2 million LY away, is the furthest object visible to the naked eye.

28 Aries (ram)
Three main stars. Gamma Arietis is a double star.

29 Pisces (fishes)
In myth, two fishes tied by a long ribbon. The constellation has no bright stars.

27 Triangulum
(triangle)
A compact pattern of three faint stars.

30 Cetus (whale)
Mira is a red-coloured star whose brightness varies. It remains visible to the naked eye for six months at a time, then fades to invisibility.

Capella (links to map, page 19)

Pleiades

Algol

Gamma Arietis

Mira

Diphda

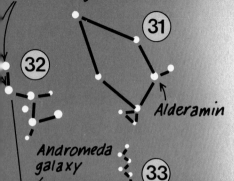

Polaris (links to map, page 13)

Pointers to Pegasus

31

32

Alderamin

Andromeda galaxy

33

26 Square of Pegasus

34

35

29

Enif

Water jug

36

31 Cepheus

In myth, Andromeda's father. Brightest star called Alderamin.

32 Cassiopeia

In myth, the wife of Cepheus. Its W-shape is very easy to spot. The two end stars can be used as pointers to Pegasus.

33 Lacerta (lizard)

A zig-zag of very faint stars; hard to find.

34 Pegasus

In Greek myth, a flying horse. Three stars and the end star of Andromeda make up the Square of Pegasus, large and easily seen though not bright.

35 Equuleus (foal)

Hard to spot, even on a very clear night.

36 Aquarius (water carrier)

Represents a man pouring water. The most obvious stars are the central four making the 'water jug'; the stars below are the stream of water from it.

Gemini to Lepus

37 Gemini (twins)

Castor is actually six stars very close together, but binoculars cannot separate them. The faint planets Uranus and Pluto were in Gemini when discovered.

38 Canis Minor
(small dog)

In myth, the smaller of the two dogs of Orion the hunter. Procyon is the eighth brightest star in the sky, and at 11 LY, among the closest to Earth.

39 Monoceros
(unicorn)

Inconspicuous and recently named (in the 17th century), but worth 'sweeping' with your binoculars for star clusters and nebulae.

40 Canis Major
(large dog)

A compact group of bright stars. Sirius (the Dog Star) is the brightest star in the sky, and only 8 LY away from Earth. Read more about it on page 29.

The twins

Castor

Pollux

37

Procyon

38

Iota Orionis

39

Lots of star clusters in this area

Sirius

40

Adara

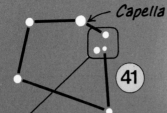

Capella

The kids

41 Auriga (charioteer)

A curving line of stars ending in a distinct but faint triangle known as 'the kids'. Capella is the sixth brightest star in the sky and 45 LY from Earth.

Alnath

Hyades star cluster

Pleiades, the Seven Sisters

Aldebaran

42 Taurus (bull)

The star Aldebaran is the bull's red eye; its head is the Hyades star cluster. Despite its name, normal eyesight can only find six stars in the 'Seven Sisters' Pleiades cluster.

Berelgeuse

Orion's belt

Rigel

Orion nebula

43 Orion

A great hunter in Greek myth. Contains more bright stars than any other constellation, including red Betelgeuse and bluish-white Rigel. Spot the Great Nebula just below the three stars of the belt.

44 Lepus (hare)

In Greek myth the hare was Orion's favourite quarry, but Arabs called the constellation 'Orion's chair'.

Columba to Microscopium

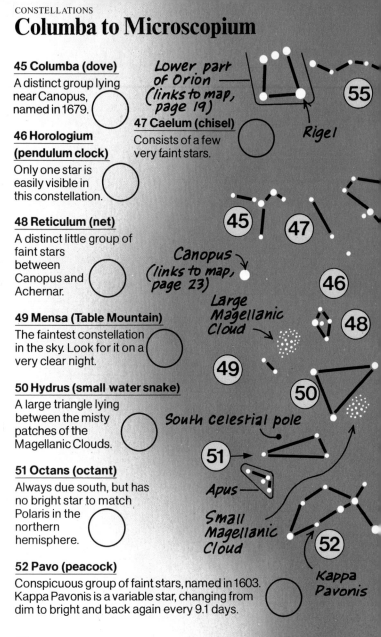

45 Columba (dove)

A distinct group lying near Canopus, named in 1679.

46 Horologium (pendulum clock)

Only one star is easily visible in this constellation.

48 Reticulum (net)

A distinct little group of faint stars between Canopus and Achernar.

49 Mensa (Table Mountain)

The faintest constellation in the sky. Look for it on a very clear night.

50 Hydrus (small water snake)

A large triangle lying between the misty patches of the Magellanic Clouds.

51 Octans (octant)

Always due south, but has no bright star to match Polaris in the northern hemisphere.

52 Pavo (peacock)

Conspicuous group of faint stars, named in 1603. Kappa Pavonis is a variable star, changing from dim to bright and back again every 9.1 days.

Lower part of Orion (links to map, page 19)

47 Caelum (chisel)

Consists of a few very faint stars.

Rigel

Canopus (links to map, page 23)

Large Magellanic Cloud

South celestial pole

Apus

Small Magellanic Cloud

Kappa Pavonis

20

53 Indus (Indian)

Lies between
Pavo and Grus.

54 Fornax (furnace)

Lies in a curve
of Eridanus.

55 Eridanus
(River Eridanus)

A winding line of
stars, named after
a mythological
river. It ends at
Achernar, the
ninth brightest
star in the sky.

56 Tucana (toucan)

A group of faint stars,
named in 1603 by
Johann Bayer.

57 Phoenix

Named in 1603 after the
mythological bird which
rises from its
own ashes.

58 Sculptor

Consists of very faint stars;
was first called
the sculptor's
workshop.

59 Piscis Austrinus
(southern fish)

Includes the star
Formalhaut, which is
24LY from Earth and
which possibly
has planets
of its own.

60 Grus (crane)

A conspicuous group,
its brightest star
is called Alnair.

61 Microscopium (microscope)

All the stars are extremely faint,
with just one easily made out.

Achernar

Fomalhaut

Alnair

Corvus to Dorado

62 Corvus (crow)
A distinct foursome of stars in a rather barren area of the sky.

63 Crater (cup)
Another group of four stars, like a fainter Corvus.

64 Antlia (air pump)
A triangle of faint stars, named in 1763.

Spica (links to map, page 12)

62

63

64

69

65

65 Vela (sail)
Part of the ancient constellation of the ship Argo. Carina and Puppis form the rest. Its outline is marked by bright stars; binoculars show many fainter ones.

66 Chameleon
Four faint stars.

67 Volans (flying fish)
Distinct group of faint stars, partly enclosed by Carina.

Crux, the southern cross (links to map, page 25)

66

67

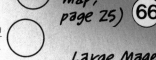

Large Magellanic Cloud

Regulus (links to map, page 13) ←

68 Sextans (sextant)
Small group of faint stars between Leo and Hydra.

69 Hydra (water snake)
The longest constellation in the sky, a sprawling line of mainly faint stars. The 'head' is a conspicuous small group of six stars. Constellation only contains one bright star, Alphard.

These three constellations used to be one large one, Argo the ship

Alphard

Procyon (links to map, page 18) ↖

Sirius (links to map, page 18) ↗

70 Pyxis (compass)
A few faint stars between Vela and Puppis.

71 Puppis (stern)
Another part of Argo, the ship in Jason's quest for the Golden Fleece. Many stars and nebulae visible in binoculars.

72 Carina (keel)
A line of stars forming the bottom of the ship Argo. At one end is Canopus, 120LY distant and the second brightest star in the sky.

Canopus

73 Pictor (easel)
Second brightest star (Beta) may have planets of its own.

74 Dorado (swordfish)
Includes the misty patch of the Large Magellanic Cloud.

Sagittarius to Crux

75 Sagittarius (archer)

A distinctive 'teapot' shape of bright stars. The misty nebula M8 is a region where stars are forming. Many other nebulae are visible with binoculars.

76 Corona Australis (southern crown)

Faint stars in a curving group.

77 Telescopium (telescope)

A group of faint stars near the 'sting' of Scorpius.

78 Ara (altar)

Lies between Alpha Centauri and the 'sting' of Scorpius.

79 Circinus (compasses)

Consists of three faint stars near Alpha Centauri; named in the 18th century.

80 Triangulum Australe (southern triangle)

An easily spotted triangle of bright stars, named in 1603. The brightest star in the group is 100 LY away.

81 Apus (bird of paradise)

An inconspicuous group of faint stars, named in 1603.

82 Musca (fly)

A constellation of faint stars next to the southern cross.

Nunki

75

M8 nebula

83

76

77

Shaula

78

80

Points to south celestial pole

81

79

82

24

83 Scorpius (scorpion)

Bright stars outline a realistic scorpion shape. Antares is a very bright red star. Binoculars show many faint star clusters.

84 Libra (scales)

A large quadrilateral of faint stars, once regarded as the claws of the scorpion.

85 Lupus (wolf)

A distinctive pattern of bright stars, stretching from Alpha Centauri to Antares.

86 Norma (level)

A group of very faint stars. The region is, however, filled with star clusters as part of Norma lies in the Milky Way.

87 Centaurus (centaur)

In myth, a creature half-man, half-horse. Alpha Centauri is the third brightest star in the sky. The faint Proxima (invisible without a telescope) is the closest star to the Sun, just 4.2 LY away.

88 Crux (southern cross)

Alpha and Gamma Crucis point the direction to the south celestial pole in Octans.

Antares

83

84

86

85

87

Alpha Centauri

Proxima Centauri

Omega Centauri star cluster

88 Gamma Crucis

Alpha Crucis

Stellar birthplaces

Stars are formed from the very tenuous hydrogen and helium gas and dust which fills space. Denser clouds of gas are called nebulae. Within them, gravitation condenses and heats up the gas until stars are formed – huge balls of hot gas, a million or more kilometres across. At the centre of a star like the Sun the temperature is about 15 million °C; it burns by nuclear reaction like a slow-motion H-bomb.

These pages show some nebulae and star clusters. There are millions more, but the ones shown here are visible as faint, fuzzy patches to the naked eye.

Some star clusters stay together, but many break up. The stars may end up single, like the Sun, or often in a pair or a trio.

▲ Lagoon nebula, M8 (page 24)

Large clouds made of hydrogen gas. The star which makes the gas glow is so deeply embedded in dust that it cannot be seen. Nebula is over 5,000LY away.

◀ Praesepe (page 13)

An easily spotted cluster, 40LY across and about 525LY from Earth. Most of the stars (about 200) are thought to be about 400 million years old. No glowing nebula of hydrogen gas is visible, even through powerful telescopes.

▲ Pleiades (page 19)

A cluster of over 250 stars formed about 60 million years ago. Often called the Seven Sisters, though only six are visible to the naked eye.

◀ Omega Centauri (page 25)

Only visible from the southern hemisphere. The cluster consists of a million stars.

Orion Nebula (pages 1 and 19)

Visible just below Orion's belt. The nebula is about 30LY across and 1,500 LY from Earth.

Types of stars

The Sun is a typical star, but not all stars are like the Sun – they vary enormously in size, colour and temperature.

Newly-formed stars, like the ones on the previous page, cover a wide range, from extremely bright and hot bluish-white stars to dim, cooler ones. The Sun is a "middle-aged" star, 5,000 million years old.

Over 50 per cent of known stars occur in pairs and many stars vary in brightness, unlike the Sun, whose light remains steady.

The colour of stars varies from an intense blue-white through yellow and orange to a dim red. The shade indicates temperature – the cooler the star, the redder it appears. This chart plots typical colours and temperatures, together with stars of each kind.

Colour				
Blue-White	White	Yellow	Orange	Red

Surface Temperature in degrees Centigrade				
25,000	10,000	6,000	4,000	3,000

Typical star				
Spica	Sirius	Sun	Arcturus	Betelgeuse

Most stars are classified into the seven groups shown below. Each group is divided into a further ten subdivisions – the Sun is spectral type G2. The types are arranged mainly by an analysis of a star's light, temperature and chemical compounds.

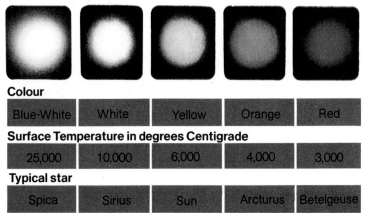

	O	B	A	F	G	K	M
30	← Iota Orionis						
25							
20		Rigel					
15			Vega	Canopus	Sun	Aldebaran	
10							Antares
5,000°C							
Type	**O**	**B**	**A**	**F**	**G**	**K**	**M**

◀ Variable star Algol (page 16)

Every three days, this star dims for ten hours but not because its light output changes. It is in fact a double star, and one of the pair periodically blocks off the light of the other, reducing the apparent brightness. The bright star is type B8, the fainter star type K.

Tick if you can spot Algol's brightness change ◯

Sirius (page 18) ▶

Sirius, 8.6 LY from Earth and spectral type A1, has a faint companion which is a white dwarf, a collapsed star core. A matchbox of matter from it would weigh 30 tonnes. You cannot see the dwarf, but should have no problem finding Sirius. Sirius is known as the 'Dog Star' as it is in Canis Major. It is the brightest star in the sky. ◯

◀ Mizar and Alcor (page 12)

Mizar, the second star in the 'handle' of the Plough, has a companion star, Alcor, which can be spotted with the naked eye. Mizar itself is a double star, but the pair can only be made out with a telescope. Alcor is arrowed in the picture. Mizar and Alcor are about 80 LY away.

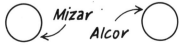
Mizar Alcor

Dying stars

A star does not shine forever. The hydrogen fuel at its centre is eventually exhausted as the 'hydrogen bomb' nuclear reaction turns it all to helium (comparable to the ash remaining after a coal or wood fire). At this point the star swells up to a hundred times its previous size. Huge stars like this are red – and some of the brightest stars in the sky are 'red giants'.

It then begins to burn helium as a nuclear fuel. Eventually, as its central nuclear fuel approaches complete exhaustion, a red giant blows up, its outer layers expanding into space. The central core collapses in upon itself, cools down and fades away. Dead stars like this are very small and very dense; their collapsed matter makes lead seem as light as a feather.

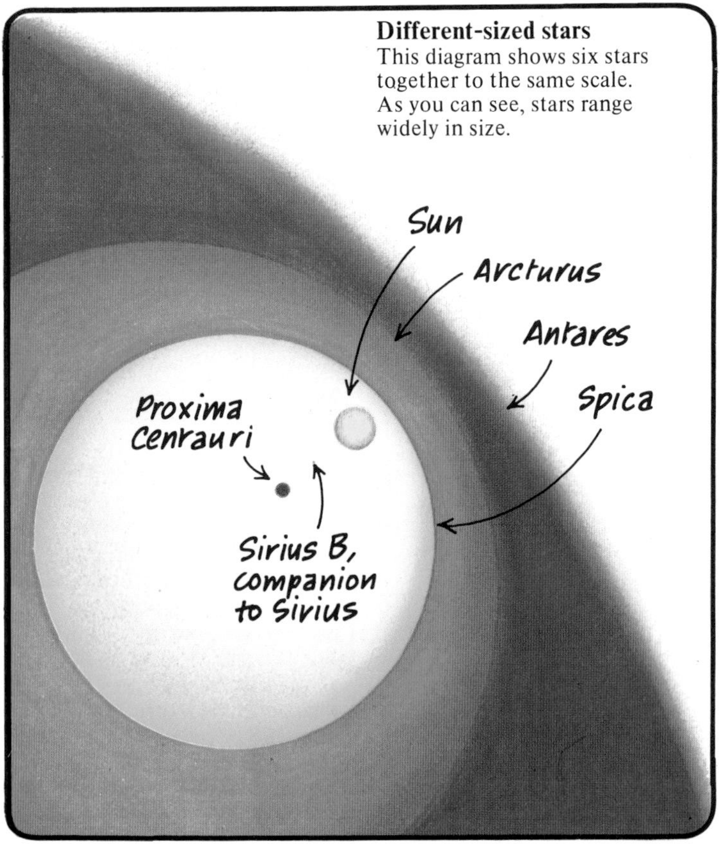

Different-sized stars
This diagram shows six stars together to the same scale. As you can see, stars range widely in size.

Sun

Arcturus

Antares

Spica

Proxima Centauri

Sirius B, companion to Sirius

◀ Mira (page 16)

The central star in the constellation of Cetus is a red giant spectral type M whose brightness varies. Over months its brightness can increase about a thousand times. It is known as a 'long-period' variable star because its brightness change takes a little under a year.

Antares (page 25) ▶

Another old red giant, about 400 million km in diameter. It has a small companion star, type B4, which can only be seen with a telescope. As you can see from the picture it is a greenish colour, but this is an optical effect caused by the contrast with bright red Antares. A cool star, Antares' surface temperature is only 3,200°C.

◀ Betelgeuse (page 19)

A red giant, easily spotted at the 'shoulder' of Orion. This picture is based on a computer analysis of temperature variations on the surface of Betelgeuse. The star is a variable – try comparing it in the sky to Aldebaran to spot slow changes in brightness. Its size varies with its brightness. At its maximum, it is nearly 700 million km across, over 500 times as large as the Sun. It is an M2 spectral type.

Galaxies

The stars you see in the sky (including the Sun) are part of a huge spiral group of 100,000 million stars, called the Galaxy.

Although you can see only a fraction of these stars, the light from the distant ones blends together to form a misty glowing band stretching right across the sky. Its name is the Milky Way and it passes through the constellations of Cassiopeia, Cygnus, Aquila, Sagittarius, Scorpius, Centaurus, Crux, Vela, Puppis, Monoceros and Perseus.

Far out beyond our own Milky Way Galaxy, there are billions more. Most are so distant that a telescope is needed to see them but three are visible to the naked eye.

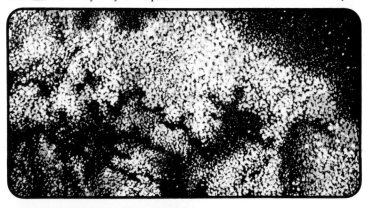

▲ Milky Way

This is a section of the Milky Way as seen through a telescope. Using binoculars, you can see many faint nebulae and star clusters within it.

◀ Coal Sack

Dust particles in space absorb starlight, producing dark 'holes' in the Milky Way. Look near Crux to find the 'Coal Sack' shown here.

◄ Magellanic Clouds
(pages 20, 21, 22, 23)

These bright misty patches, only visible from the southern hemisphere, were first spotted by the explorer Ferdinand Magellan in 1521. They are smaller than our own galaxy and are the closest galaxies to the Milky Way. Neither has a distinctive shape, which is unusual – larger galaxies are spiral or oval in shape.

Large Magellanic Cloud ↘
(top picture)

Small Magellanic → *Cloud*

◄ Andromeda Galaxy
(page 17)

To the naked eye it looks like a faint blur. It is 2.2 million LY away and is the most distant object you can see without binoculars or a telescope. Its spiral shape is similar to that of the Milky Way. Galaxies group together in clusters. Andromeda is a member of the Local Group, along with the Milky Way, the Magellanic Clouds and about 25 other galaxies.

Empire of the Sun

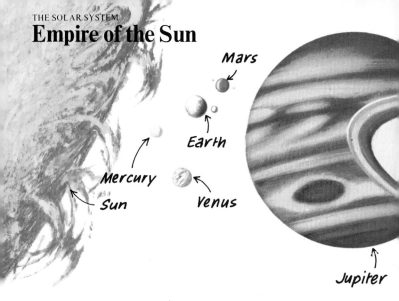

On a clear night, you will probably see one or more bright points of light which are not marked on the star maps. These are the planets.

The planets gradually change their positions against the background stars, so they cannot be marked on the constellation maps.

After each planet's description on the following pages there is a table showing which constellation it is moving through during the next few years. Apart from Uranus, Neptune and Pluto, the planets appear very bright, and once you have located the constellations you

Planetary fact-finder

Planet	Diameter	Average distance from Sun
Mercury	4,880 km	58 million km
Venus	12,100 km	108 million km
Earth	12,756 km	150 million km
Mars	6,794 km	228 million km
Jupiter	142,800 km	778 million km
Saturn	120,000 km	1,429 million km
Uranus	51,800 km	2,875 million km
Neptune	48,600 km	4,500 million km
Pluto	2,400 km	5,900 million km

Planets and satellites all shown to the same scale

Uranus

Neptune

Pluto

Saturn

cannot miss them.

Like the Earth, the other planets circle the Sun. They have no light of their own, and only shine because they reflect sunlight.

All the planets revolve around the Sun in the same direction, and their orbits lie nearly in the same plane like the tracks on an LP record. As a result, all the planets seem to move through the same group of constellations, the zodiac. The zodiac consists of Pisces, Aries, Taurus, Gemini, Cancer, Leo, Virgo, Libra, Scorpius, Sagittarius, Capricornus and Aquarius.

Time to orbit Sun (year)	Time to rotate (day)	Number of satellites
88 days	59 days	None
225 days	243 days	None
365.3 days	23 hrs 56 mins	1 (the Moon)
687 days	24 hrs 37 mins	2
11.9 years	9 hrs 50 mins	16
29.5 years	10 hrs 14 mins	17
84 years	17 hrs, 14 mins	15
165 years	18 hrs	8
248 years	6 days 10 hrs	1

Mercury

The diameter of Mercury, closest planet to the Sun, is only 50 per cent larger than that of the Moon. It has no atmosphere and during its day the Sun bakes its surface up to 430°C. At night it becomes very cold (–170°C). Mercury is heavily cratered like the Moon, and has long ridges where it has shrunk slightly, like an old apple. This picture is based on photographs taken by the Mariner 10 spacecraft in March 1974.

Mercury is not very easy to spot. Being always close to the Sun, it is only seen low on the horizon in the twilight glow.

Mercury – when and where to look

Year	East before sunrise	Year	West after sunset
1992	August, December	1992	March, June
1993	April, November	1993	February, June
1994	November, July	1994	May
1995	July, October	1995	January, May
1996	June, October	1996	April, December
1997	January, September	1997	April, July

Venus

Venus is almost as large as Earth, but its atmosphere is a hundred times thicker and composed of choking carbon dioxide. This thick blanket makes Venus's surface very hot – 480°C – hot enough to melt lead. Venus is veiled by continuous clouds, probably made of sulphuric acid droplets. Radar experiments and space probes have shown that its surface has craters, mountains and valleys.

Venus is the brightest object in the sky after the Sun and Moon. It appears either as the 'Evening Star' after sunset, or the 'Morning Star' before sunrise.

Venus – when and where to look

Year	East before sunrise	Year	West after sunset
1992	January-April	1992	August-December
1993	April-November	1993	January-March
1994	November-December	1994	March-October
1995	January-July	1995	October-December
1996	July-December	1996	January-May
1997	January-February	1997	May-December

Mars

Mars is a rocky planet, half the diameter of Earth. It has a very thin atmosphere, of unbreathable carbon dioxide, and has no liquid water on the surface. Its entire surface, apart from icy polar caps, is a dry red desert. Despite its small size, Mars has canyons and volcanoes larger than any on Earth: one volcano, Olympus Mons, is 25km high and 500km across. Mars has two small moons, Phobos and Deimos.

This picture is based on photographs taken by American spaceprobes which have landed on the planet and sampled the soil and air. Mars appears in the sky as a bright, red 'star.'

Mars – where and when to look

Year	Months visible	Constellation	Page
1992	August	Taurus	19
	September-December	Gemini	18
1993	January-April	Gemini	18
	May	Cancer	13
1994	September	Gemini	18
	October-November	Cancer	13
1995	January-February, May	Leo	13
	March-April	Cancer	13
1996	November-December	Leo	13
1997	January-March, June	Virgo	12
	April-May	Leo	13

Jupiter is the largest planet, but despite its size, it spins faster than the Earth. Its day lasts less than 10 hours.

The stripes visible through a telescope are cloud layers. Jupiter's most noticeable feature is the Great Red Spot, shown below left. This may be an enormous hurricane that has been blowing for at least 300 years. It was first spotted in 1664 and was thought to be a volcano.

Jupiter appears as a bright yellowish-white point of light, brighter than any of the stars. On the left is the Great Red Spot compared in size to the Earth.

Jupiter – where and when to look

Year	Months visible	Constellation	Page
1992	January-May	Leo	13
1993	January-May	Virgo	12
1994	March-June	Libra	25
1995	April-July	Ophiuchus	14
1996	May-August	Sagittarius	24
1997	June-October	Capricornus	14

Saturn

Saturn, the second largest planet, consists almost entirely of substances that are gases on Earth: ammonia, methane, hydrogen and helium. Inside Saturn enormous gravity compresses these into liquids.

Saturn is famous for its rings. These consist of billions of ice particles, all orbiting Saturn like miniature moons. Saturn has 17 moons; the largest Titan, has orange clouds.

The telescope view above shows Saturn and its rings. It appears to the naked eye as a bright yellow 'star.' Its rings are only visible through a telescope.

Saturn – where and when to look

Year	Months visible	Constellation	Page
1992	May-November	Capricornus	14
1993	June-November	Capricornus	14
1994	June-December	Aquarius	17
1995	June-August	Pisces	16
	September-December	Aquarius	17
1996	June-December	Pisces	16
1997	January, June-December	Pisces	16

Uranus, Neptune, Pluto

The three outer planets are not visible to the naked eye and little was known about them until the Voyager 2 spacecraft flew past Uranus and Neptune sending us detailed photographs of the planets and their rings and moons.

▼ Uranus

Discovered in 1781 by William Herschel. In 1986 the Voyager 2 spacecraft photographed Uranus, its rings and 15 moons.

Neptune ▶

Bluish in colour, this planet is similar to Uranus in size. It has two satellites, Nereid and Triton. Triton is one of the largest satellites in the Solar System, being 2,720km in diameter.

Pluto ▶

These two pictures were taken in 1930. One of the 'stars' (arrowed) moved, showing that it was a planet. Only powerful telescopes can show Pluto and its large moon, Charon. Pluto's orbit passes inside that of Neptune, and until 1999, Neptune will be the outermost planet.

Comets

Comets are balls of ice, dust and rock, drifting in huge elongated orbits that extend far into space, even beyond the orbit of Pluto. As a comet nears the Sun, the heat turns the ice into a mini-atmosphere, that streams out into a tail extending for millions of miles. Sometimes a comet is large and bright enough to be seen without binoculars, though most are only visible through telescopes.

Tail of gas and dust – can be millions of miles long

Nucleus – made of rocks and ice

Coma – made of gases

◄ A spectacular long-tailed comet is quite a rare sight. Fainter comets have a coma but no tail.

This picture shows Ikeya-Seki, a comet which appeared in 1965

Halley's Comet

Of the comets which reappear regularly, the brightest is Halley's Comet. It reappears every 76 years, so will next appear some time during 2061 or 2062.

Asteroids

Between the orbits of Mars and Jupiter there are thousands of rocks, called asteroids, orbiting the Sun. They range in diameter from 1,003km downwards. Even the largest are too faint to be seen with the unaided eye. The early Solar System contained only asteroid-like rocks. Most of them accumulated to make the planets, leaving the remainder orbiting in a belt between Mars and Jupiter.

Asteroid Belt

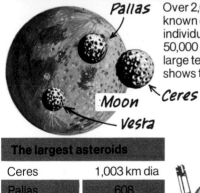

Pallas

Moon

Ceres

Vesta

Over 2,000 asteroids have precisely known orbits, and have been given individual names. It is estimated that 50,000 asteroids are visible with a large telescope. The picture on the left shows the three largest compared in size with the Moon.

The largest asteroids	
Ceres	1,003 km dia
Pallas	608
Vesta	538
Hygeia	450
Euphrosyne	370

Pioneer 10, the first spaceprobe to cross the Asteroid Belt, on its way to Jupiter

The Moon

The Moon is Earth's only natural satellite. It is an airless, dry and small world, 3,476km in diameter (about a quarter the size of the Earth). This is large for a satellite, however, and many astronomers regard the Earth and Moon as a double-planet system,

(Pluto is another "double planet"). The Moon's surface is covered with round craters, up to 250km across, which were blasted out by asteroids and meteorites millions of years ago. The Moon has high mountains, some almost 10,000 metres high.

Here are nineteen lunar features which are easy to spot. You will need binoculars to see ones marked ★

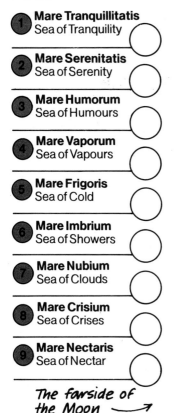

1 Mare Tranquillitatis
Sea of Tranquility

2 Mare Serenitatis
Sea of Serenity

3 Mare Humorum
Sea of Humours

4 Mare Vaporum
Sea of Vapours

5 Mare Frigoris
Sea of Cold

6 Mare Imbrium
Sea of Showers

7 Mare Nubium
Sea of Clouds

8 Mare Crisium
Sea of Crises

9 Mare Nectaris
Sea of Nectar

The farside of the Moon ⟶

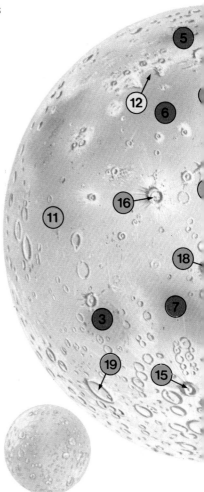

The dark patches spread over large areas are plains of solidified lava. Early astronomers thought they were seas and oceans and they still bear the Latin names 'mare' (sea), 'oceanus' (ocean) and 'sinus' (bay).

The Moon always keeps the same side to Earth. It turns on its own axis in exactly the same time as it takes to orbit the Earth, $27\frac{1}{3}$ days. No-one knew what the other side looked like until spaceprobes took pictures in the 1950s and 60s.

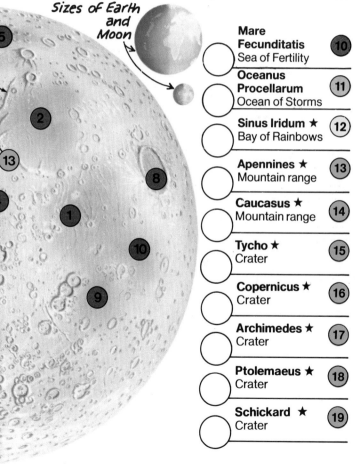

Sizes of Earth and Moon

Mare Fecunditatis Sea of Fertility (10)

Oceanus Procellarum Ocean of Storms (11)

Sinus Iridum ★ Bay of Rainbows (12)

Apennines ★ Mountain range (13)

Caucasus ★ Mountain range (14)

Tycho ★ Crater (15)

Copernicus ★ Crater (16)

Archimedes ★ Crater (17)

Ptolemaeus ★ Crater (18)

Schickard ★ Crater (19)

Phases of the Moon

The Full Moon is the brightest object in the sky after the Sun, but it emits no light of its own. Like the planets, it merely reflects sunlight. As the Moon orbits Earth, different amounts of the sunlit half are visible, so the lit shape (called the phase) changes. The phases repeat every 29½ days. Although it looks so bright, the Moon only reflects about seven per cent of the sunlight falling on it–its surface is quite dark.

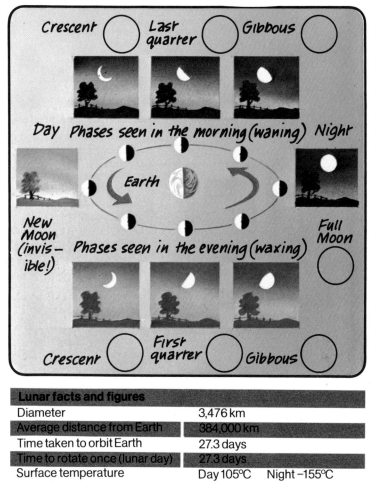

Lunar facts and figures	
Diameter	3,476 km
Average distance from Earth	384,000 km
Time taken to orbit Earth	27.3 days
Time to rotate once (lunar day)	27.3 days
Surface temperature	Day 105°C Night −155°C

Eclipses

The New Moon sometimes passes in front of the Sun, cutting off its light. This is called an eclipse of the Sun. When Full, the Moon sometimes passes into the shadow of the Earth. There is little light to reflect, so the Moon dims to a very faint copper colour. This is called an eclipse of the Moon.

The two diagrams on this page show how eclipses occur, but they are not to scale.

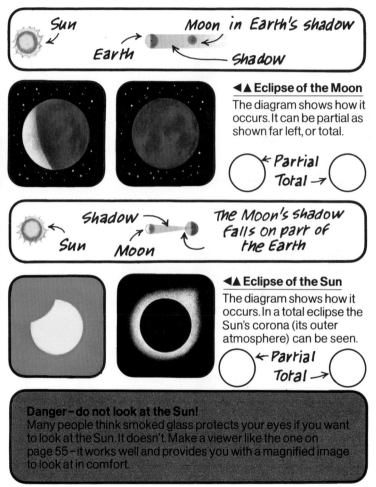

◀▲ Eclipse of the Moon
The diagram shows how it occurs. It can be partial as shown far left, or total.

← Partial
Total →

◀▲ Eclipse of the Sun
The diagram shows how it occurs. In a total eclipse the Sun's corona (its outer atmosphere) can be seen.

← Partial
Total →

Danger – do not look at the Sun!
Many people think smoked glass protects your eyes if you want to look at the Sun. It doesn't. Make a viewer like the one on page 55 – it works well and provides you with a magnified image to look at in comfort.

Meteors

Between planets there is assorted debris ranging from enormous rocks to tiny grains of dust. These are called meteoroids and can move at up to 70km per second.

Meteors

When a meteoroid collides with the Earth's atmosphere, friction heats it white-hot and it shines briefly as a meteor or 'shooting star' before it burns up.

A really bright one is called a fireball; it usually leaves a briefly glowing trail.

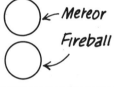

← Meteor

Fireball

Meteor showers

Most small meteoroids are the remains of broken-up comets. As the Earth crosses various comet orbits there are spectacular showers of meteors.

The effect of perspective makes meteors seem to spread out from a point in the sky, just as a road seems to spread from a distant point. Meteor showers are named after the constellation in which the spreading-out point, or radiant lies.

Most meteors become visible some distance away from the radiant, so when spotting a meteor shower do not look directly at the radiant. When you see a meteor, trace its path backwards in the sky. If this line goes through the constellation containing the radiant you will have seen a 'shower' meteor.

Meteorites

If a meteor crashes into the ground it is called a meteorite. To see one land is very, very rare so tick off the spotting circles if you see meteorites in a museum – many have collections.

▲ Stony meteorites

There are two main types of meteorites – stony and iron. The technical name for a stony one is an aerolite. Often covered with a smooth black crust.

Iron meteorite ▶

Known as a siderite. Examination under a microscope reveals a peculiar criss-cross pattern. A million-tonne siderite blasted a 1,200 metre-wide hole in Arizona 20,000 years ago.

Important meteor showers

Dates visible	Name	Radiant	
January 1-6	Quadrantids	Boötes (page 12)	◯
April 19-24	Lyrids	Lyra (page 15)	◯
May 1-8	Eta Aquarids	Aquarius (page 17)	◯
July 25 – August 18	Perseids	Perseus (page 16)	◯
October 16-21	Orionids	Orion (page 19)	◯
October 20 – November 30	Taurids	Taurus (page 19)	◯
December 7-15	Geminids	Gemini (page 18)	◯

Other sky sights

In addition to the stars and planets, there are other things to spot nearer the Earth. Note that aurorae can rarely be seen from tropical latitudes; zodiacal light cannot be seen from polar latitudes.

◄ Aurora Borealis/Australis

Known as Borealis in northern hemisphere, Australis in south. Shimmering curtain effect is caused by radiation from Sun striking particles in Earth's upper atmosphere.

Zodiacal light ►

Faint cone of light caused by sunlight reflecting off dust particles in space. Best seen from tropics. Glow passes through the constellations of the zodiac.

◄ Night-time vapour trails

The upper atmosphere remains in sunlight for a short period after sunset on the ground below. Aircraft vapour trails glow faintly as the ice crystals of which they are composed reflect the Sun.

Halo round the Moon ►

Ice particles in the upper atmosphere cause this effect. Usually one ring, but sometimes two, can be seen. Normally silvery-white in colour. Very occasionally, haloes can look like very pale rainbows.

Artificial satellites

Since the Space Age began in 1957 with the launch of Sputnik I, thousands of artifical satellites have been launched to orbit Earth. The largest satellites (and discarded rockets in orbit) can be seen with the unaided eye. They look like slow but steadily moving points of white light. Beware of mistaking aircraft for satellites. Aircraft generally have coloured identification lights, and their engines are usually audible on a still night, while satellites are silent.

Artificial satellite ▶

Some newspapers carry details of the time that satellites are due, though there are so many that an hour's watch will usually enable you to spot one. As the satellite passes into the Earth's shadow it will be eclipsed, fading out of sight.

◀ Flashing satellite

This is not a light fitted on board, but the result of the satellite spinning in orbit. Sunlight reflects off different parts causing the flashing effect as it slowly moves across the sky.

Unidentified flying objects ▶

UFOs are unexplained moving lights – some people think they are spaceships from other worlds. About 40 sightings are reported across the world every day, but most are hoaxes or due to confusion with ordinary objects.

Taking photographs

You can take photographs of the sky if you have a camera with a 'Brief Time' (B) setting. When set to this, the shutter stays open as long as you keep your finger pressed on the release button.

If the camera has aperture and focus controls, use the smallest f number (2.8 is common) and focus on infinity (∞ is the symbol used).

Colour slide film is best. If you use negative or black and white film, explain to the processing laboratory that they are star pictures otherwise they will think there is nothing on the film and give you no prints.

Wide aperture

B setting

Cable release

▲ Setting up the camera

The camera must not move throughout the exposure. Prop the camera on a wall if you can, or better still, mount it on a tripod and use a cable release to press the button.

Star trails ▶

Point the camera at Polaris (or Octans in southern skies). Keep the shutter open several minutes (or hours). You should get a result like the one shown here as the polar stars rotate in the sky.

Constellation legends

Most of the prominent constellations have names taken from ancient Greek myths and legends. Many of these are based on the stories of still older civilizations.

On this page you can see just one group of constellations and their story. As you can see, the Greeks certainly used their imaginations when they related star patterns to human and animal shapes! There are many others – try finding out about them from an encyclopedia.

The Greeks saw the stars shown here, visible on January and February nights, as a giant display dominated by the great hunter Orion. He is facing a charging bull, Taurus, with a raised club and lion-skin shield. Behind him are his two faithful hunting dogs, Canis Major and Canis Minor. Unnoticed at his feet is his favourite quarry, Lepus the hare.

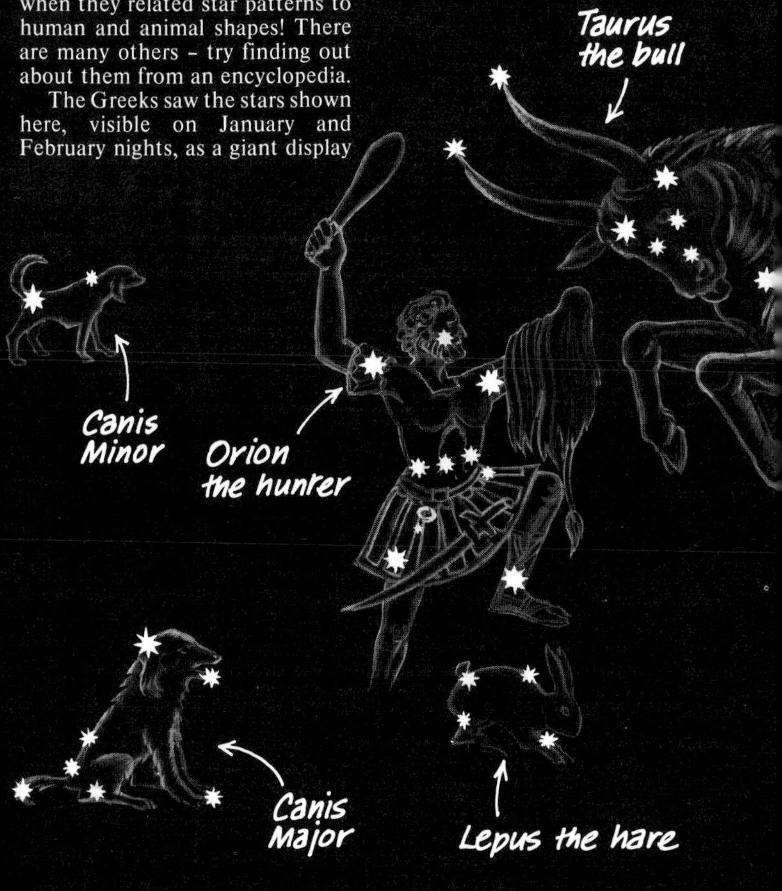

Taurus the bull

Canis Minor

Orion the hunter

Canis Major

Lepus the hare

Constellation quiz

Name each constellation and fill in the missing star in each pattern. Constellation names are shown at the bottom of the page.

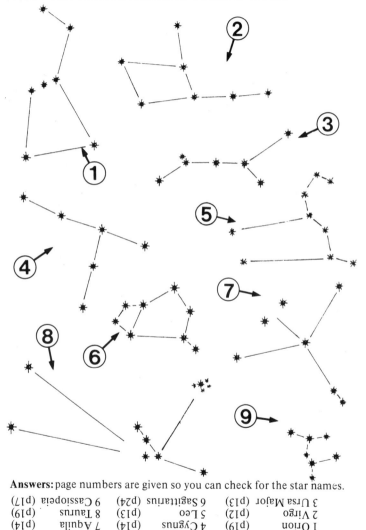

Answers: page numbers are given so you can check for the star names.

1 Orion (p19)	5 Leo (p13)	9 Cassiopeia (p17)
2 Virgo (p12)	6 Sagittarius (p24)	
3 Ursa Major (p13)	7 Aquila (p14)	
4 Cygnus (p14)	8 Taurus (p19)	

54

Make a Sun-spotter

This is the only way to look at the Sun safely. Looking at it directly will blind you; filters or smoked glass are not safe either.

The Sun-spotter takes about 30 minutes to make and its results are excellent. Prop the spotter on a chair to get a good steady image.

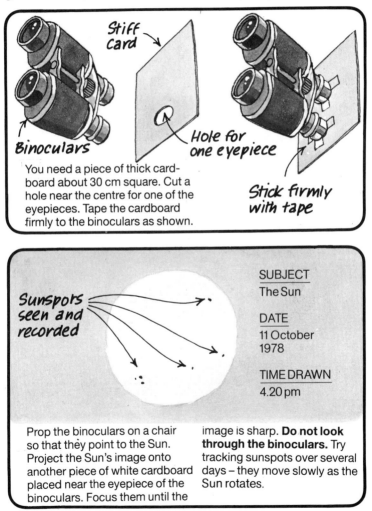

Stiff card

Binoculars

Hole for one eyepiece

You need a piece of thick cardboard about 30 cm square. Cut a hole near the centre for one of the eyepieces. Tape the cardboard firmly to the binoculars as shown.

Stick firmly with tape

Sunspots seen and recorded

SUBJECT
The Sun

DATE
11 October 1978

TIME DRAWN
4.20 pm

Prop the binoculars on a chair so that they point to the Sun. Project the Sun's image onto another piece of white cardboard placed near the eyepiece of the binoculars. Focus them until the image is sharp. **Do not look through the binoculars.** Try tracking sunspots over several days – they move slowly as the Sun rotates.

Interplanetary puzzles

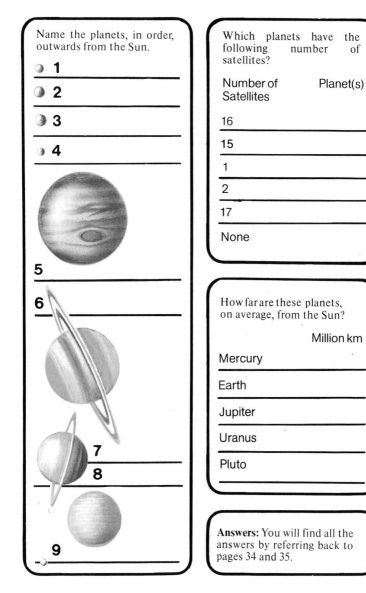

Name the planets, in order, outwards from the Sun.

1 _____

2 _____

3 _____

4 _____

5

6 _____

7

8 _____

9 _____

Which planets have the following number of satellites?

Number of Satellites	Planet(s)
16	
15	
1	
2	
17	
None	

How far are these planets, on average, from the Sun?

	Million km
Mercury	
Earth	
Jupiter	
Uranus	
Pluto	

Answers: You will find all the answers by referring back to pages 34 and 35.

Pronunciation guide

The names of many of the stars and constellations are tongue-twisting to pronounce. In this list of the more difficult ones, emphasise the syllable printed in bold as you speak to get the right pronunciation.

Constellations

Andromeda
AN-DROM-EDA

Aquila
AK-WILL-AH

Aries
AIR-RIZ

Boötes
BOH-**OH**-TEZ

Caelum
SEE-LUM

Camelopardalis
KAM-ELL-OH-**PARD**-A-LIS

Canes Venatici
KAN-AYZ VEN-**AT**-I-SEE

Cassiopeia
KASS-EE-OH-**PEE**-AH

Cepheus
SEE-FEE-US

Cetus
SEE-TUS

Circinus
SUR-SIN-US

Coma Berenices
KOH-MAH
BERR-REN-**NICE**-EZ

Corona Australis
KOR-**ROH**-NAH
OST-**TRAH**-LIS

Corona Borealis
KOR-**ROH**-NAH
BOR-REE-**AY**-LIS

Equuleus
EK-**KWOO**-LEE-US

Lacerta
LASS-**SER**-TAH

Lepus
LEP-PUSS

Libra
LEE-BRAH

Monoceros
MON-**NOSS**-ER-OS

Ophiuchus
OFF-EE-**OO**-KUS

Orion
OR-**RY**-ON

Pisces
PY-SEEZ

Piscis Austrinus
PY-SIS **OST**-RIN-IS

Vulpecula
VULL-**PEK**-YOO-LAH

Stars

Achernar
A-**KER**-NAR

Albireo
ALBI-**REE**-OH

Aldebaran
AL-**DEB**-AH-RAN

Alpha Centauri
AL-FA SEN-**TOR**-EE.

Antares
AN-**TAR**-EEZ

Betelgeuse
BEE-TELL-GURZ

Dubhe
DOOB-EE

Fomalhaut
FOH-MAL-OH

Iota Orionis
I-**OH**-TA OR-**RY**-ON-IS

Mizar
MY-ZAR

Polaris
POE-**LAR**-IS

Procyon
PRO-**SY**-ON

Rasalgethi
RAH-SAL-**JETH**-EE

Planetariums

A planetarium is like a circular cinema with a domed ceiling. The audience sees images of stars, planets and other wonders of the night sky displayed on the dome by a special projector.

The projector shown is typical of the sort you will see in a good planetarium. Running around the 'horizon' of the dome is a silhouetted skyline to increase the illusion of actually watching the sky.

Some major cities have planetariums – among them London and New York.

Star dome

Projector

Main globe projects fixed star images

Solar System projector

Map reference projector

Milky Way projector

Projector rotates about its central axis

Top globe projects northern hemisphere stars, the bottom one southern hemisphere stars

58

Here are some definitions of terms used in this book.

Asteroid One of the many thousands of lumps of rock orbiting the Sun between Mars and Jupiter. Some asteroids do not stay in these areas – some pass very near the Earth.

Big Bang Name given to the initial explosion of matter which scientists think was the beginning of the Universe.

Binary Two stars orbiting round each other. Usually too close to be seen separately, except with binoculars or telescope.

Eclipse When one object moves into the shadow of another, it is eclipsed. A lunar eclipse occurs when the Moon moves into the Earth's shadow. In an eclipse of the Sun, the Sun is hidden by the Moon for a brief period.

Galaxy A giant group of stars. The Milky Way Galaxy contains about 100,000 million stars.

Hemisphere One half of a sphere. The Earth's northern hemisphere is the half north of the equator.

Light Year Distance travelled by light in a year. The speed of light is just over 300,000km a second, so a light year is 9.5 million million km.

Local group of galaxies Like stars, galaxies tend to collect in groups. The Milky Way is one of a group of about 30 galaxies.

Meteoroid A piece of rock or a dust particle flying free in space. Called a meteor if it enters the Earth's atmosphere; if it hits the ground, a meteorite. Millions of meteors collide with the atmosphere every year.

Nebula Cloud of dust and gas between the stars where new stars are formed.

Orbit Curving path taken by a celestial object when it revolves around another, for example, the Earth around the Sun.

Phases Different shapes that the Moon and some planets seem to have as differing amounts of their sunlit side are seen.

Radiant Central point from which, by the effect of perspective, a shower of meteors seems to come.

Satellite Small celestial object orbiting around another, such as the Moon around the Earth. Artificial satellites orbit the Earth in their hundreds.

Star Luminous ball of gas, powered by the energy of nuclear fusion. Surface temperatures range from 3,000°C – 50,000°C.

Sunspot A cool area on the surface of the Sun. Because it is cooler it looks darker, even though it is actually a scorching 4,000°C.

White dwarf Tiny remains of a once much larger star. Its matter has collapsed to a point at which a spoonful would weigh many tons.

Scorecard

After a night's spotting, write the date next to the objects seen in this scorecard. Keep a record of your nightly scores. The letter N or S next to a score shows that the object is visible only from the northern or southern hemisphere. Other objects, like meteorites, will usually be seen in museums, so score if you see them there.

	Score	Date seen		Score	Date seen
Artificial satellites Flashing satellite	20		Capricornus	15	
Satellite	10		Carina	10S	
Satellite eclipse	15		Cassiopeia	5N	
Aurora Australis	25S		Centaurus	5S	
Aurora Borealis	25N		Cepheus	15N	
Comet	40		Cetus	15	
Constellations Andromeda	10		Chameleon	20S	
Antlia	20S		Circinus	20S	
Apus	15S		Columba	15S	
Aquarius	15		Coma Berenices	20	
Aquila	10		Corona Australis	10S	
Ara	15S		Corona Borealis	10	
Aries	10		Corvus	10	
Auriga	10		Crater	15	
Boötes	5		Crux	5S	
Caelum	20S		Cygnus	5	
Camelopardalis	20N		Delphinus	10	
Cancer	15		Dorado	20S	
Canes Venatici	15N		Draco	10N	
Canis Major	5		Equuleus	20	
Canis Minor	10		Eridanus	10	

	Score	Date seen		Score	Date seen
Fornax	25S		Pegasus	10	
Gemini	5		Perseus	10N	
Grus	15S		Phoenix	15S	
Hercules	15		Pictor	20S	
Horologium	20S		Pisces	20	
Hydra	10		Piscis Austrinus	15	
Hydrus	15S		Puppis	15	
Indus	20S		Pyxis	20S	
Lacerta	20N		Reticulum	15S	
Leo	5		Sagitta	15	
Leo Minor	15N		Sagittarius	5	
Lepus	10		Scorpius	5	
Libra	15		Sculptor	25S	
Lupus	15S		Scutum	20	
Lynx	20N		Serpens Caput & Cauda	15	
Lyra	5		Sextans	25	
Mensa	25S		Taurus	10	
Microscopium	25S		Telescopium	20S	
Monoceros	20		Triangulum	15	
Musca	15S		Triangulum Australe	10S	
Norma	20S		Tucana	15S	
Octans	20S		Ursa Major	5N	
Ophiuchus	10		Ursa Minor	10N	
Orion	5		Vela	10S	
Pavo	15S		Virgo	10	

	Score	Date seen		Score	Date seen
Volans	20**S**		Humorum	15	
Vulpecula	20		Imbrium	10	
Eclipses: Lunar Partial	30		Nectaris	15	
Total	40		Nubium	15	
Solar Partial	35		Serenitatis	10	
Total	50		Tranquillitatis	10	
Meteors Fireball	30		Vaporum	15	
Meteor	10		Oceanus Procellarum	5	
Aerolite	10		Ptolemaeus	20	
Siderite	10		Phases of the Moon First quarter	5	
Eta Aquarids	20		Full	5	
Geminids	20		Last quarter	5	
Lyrids	20		Waning crescent	5	
Orionids	20		Waning gibbous	5	
Perseids	15		Waxing crescent	5	
Quadrantids	20		Waxing gibbous	5	
Taurids	20		Schickard	15	
Moon Archimedes	20		Sinus Iridum	15	
Caucasus	20		Tycho	15	
Copernicus	15		**Nebulae and star clusters**		
Halo	15		Lagoon nebula	20	
Appenines	10		Omega Centauri	10**S**	
Mare Crisium	5		Orion nebula	10	
Foecunditatis	10		Pleiades	10**N**	
Frigoris	15		Praesepe	20	